The Grumpy Troll

by Liza Charlesworth
illustrated by John Lund

ISBN: 979-8-225-02083-5

Publisher: Tara Welty
Creative Director: Tannaz Fassihi; Designer: Cynthia Ng

1 2 3 4 5 6 7 8 9 10 68 34 33 32 31 30 29 28 27 26 25

Made in Jiaxing City, China. First printing, August 2025.

SCHOLASTIC

Hi, reader! This book tells the tale of Trevor.
Trevor was a blue troll with big, fluffy hair.
He made his home in a snug cottage
in the middle of a thick, green forest.
Trevor had stacks and stacks of books.
He had paints and games and puzzles.

But did Trevor feel happy? No, not a bit. Each day, he stomped through the forest with a mean scowl on his face. Grrrrrrr! Did he greet any of the cool creatures that he passed along the way? Nope! You see, Trevor was a grumpy troll.

One morning, while Trevor was taking his walk, he spotted a green witch in a tall black hat. The witch was making a brew and chanting. She gave Trevor a wave, but he just frowned. So, she went back to stirring her pot and saying, “Bubble, fubble! Mumbo, gumbo!”

The witch kept chanting those words until—
CRASH! A huge bolt of lightning flashed
in the sky and it started to rain very hard.
The rain fell on Trevor and he got soaked.
"Grrrrr!" Trevor growled. "I must say
this day is off to a VERY bad start.
I think that witch put a curse on me!"

Drip, drop! Drip, drop! Drip, drop!
At last, all of the rain stopped and
the sun poked through the clouds.
But did Trevor feel better? No way!
"The light is too bright!" he complained.
"I think that witch put a curse on me."

What did that grumpy troll do next? Stomp, stomp! He walked to the park. "I need to go on the swings right now!" he hollered. But there was a long line, and Trevor did NOT like to take turns.

What was Trevor's next stop? The big slide!
The slide was tall, loopy, and very spooky.
Did Trevor slip down it and smile? Nope.
You see, the slide had a note that said:
Please do not ride. Closed for repairs.

“Darn! That’s just not fair,” Trevor whined. “I think that witch put a curse on me.” There was just one place left for that grumpy troll to go: Skelly’s Snack Shack. “A yummy treat is the ONLY thing that will make me feel better,” he howled. So, off he went. Stomp, stomp!

At Skelly's Snack Shack, Trevor stepped up to the window and he placed his order: an ice-cream cone with a scoop of peach, a scoop of beet, and a scoop of dill pickle. But when he opened up his cranky mouth to take a big bite—Plop, plop, plop! The three scoops landed on his shirt!

"I am having such BAD luck!" he grumbled.
"I just know that witch put a curse on me!"
In a rage, Trevor went home to clean his shirt.
Spin, spin, spin! Round and round it went.
But when he took the shirt out of the dryer—
Oh, drat! It had shrunken to a doll's size!

“I cannot take it anymore!” Trevor fumed.
“This is the most HORRIBLE day I ever had.
I am certain that witch put a curse on me.
There is just one thing to do: Go yell at her!”
But as Trevor stomped through the forest,
he began to sneeze: “ACHOO, ACHOO!”

By the time Trevor reached the green witch, he had never, ever felt as sick or as mad. “WE MEET AGAIN, WITCH!” screamed Trevor. “YOU NEED TO REMOVE THE CURSE YOU PUT ON ME OR ELSE—ACHOO, ACHOO!” But the green witch did not flinch a bit. She just gave him a rag to wipe his nose.

Then she replied, “You have it all wrong.
I am a nice witch and I don’t do curses.
It is true that I did stir this pot and chant,
‘Bubble, fubble! Mumbo, gumbo!’
But that’s because I was making soup.
And based on your loud sneezing,
I think you need a huge bowl of it.”

“ACHOO! YOU MEAN TO TELL ME YOU DID NOT PUT A CURSE ON ME?” yelled Trevor. “THEN WHY DID I HAVE A HORRIBLE DAY?”
“It was horrible because you were mean,” she replied. “When you grump and frown and stomp around, things do NOT go well.”

That made Trevor stop yelling and start thinking.
She was right. Being mean just wasn't working.
"OK. I will start being a sweet—ACHOO!—troll."
"Sounds like a VERY wise plan," said the witch.
"Now, sit down and have a big bowl of hot soup."
Mmmmmm. The soup made Trevor feel better.
And being nice made his whole life nice, too!